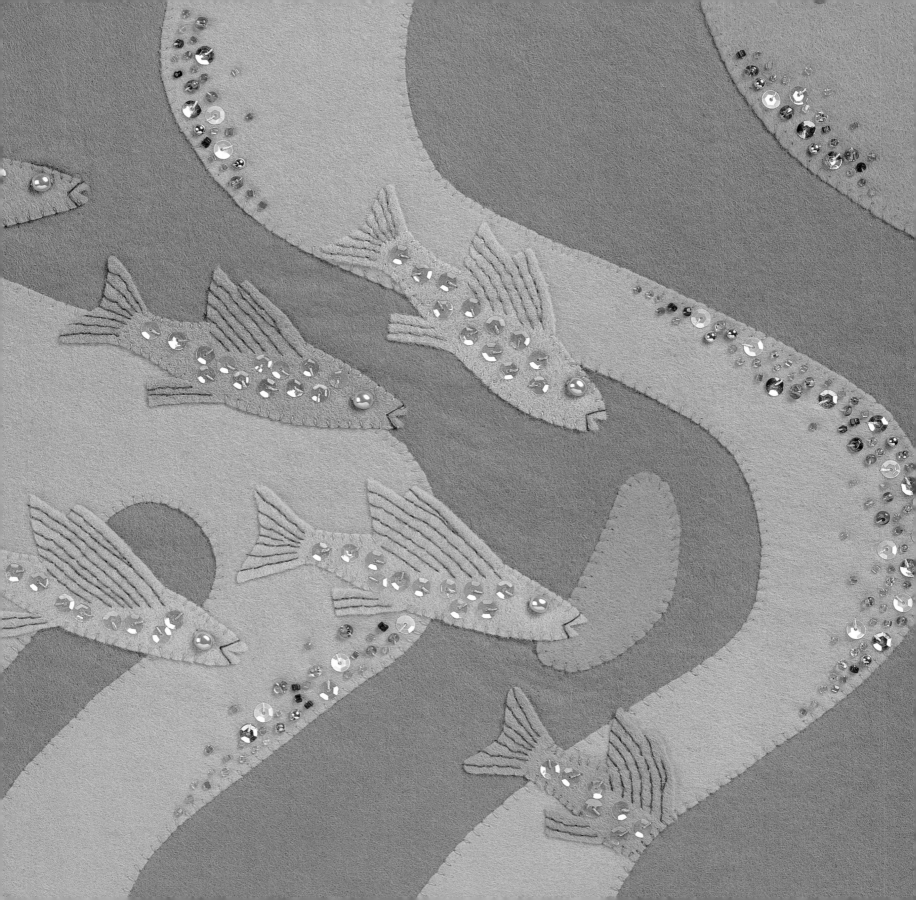

Secret
Seahorse

For Benedict, with lots of love — S. B.

For Jack William Leese — C. B.

Barefoot Books
124 Walcot Street
Bath
BA1 5BG

This book was typeset in 24pt Goudy Infant Regular
The illustrations were prepared in antique fabrics and felt
with sequins, buttons, beads and assorted bric-a-brac.

Graphic design by Barefoot Books, Bath
Colour transparencies by Jonathan Fisher Photography, Bath
Colour separation by Bright Arts, Singapore
Printed and bound in Singapore by Tien Wah Press Pte Ltd

This book has been printed on 100% acid-free paper

ISBN 1-84148-703-1

British Cataloguing-in-Publication Data: a catalogue
record for this book is available from the British library

1 3 5 7 9 8 6 4 2

Secret Seahorse

written by Stella Blackstone

illustrated by Clare Beaton

Barefoot Books
Celebrating Art and Story

I saw a secret seahorse deep down in the sea.

I tried to swim beside him. He was too quick for me.

He swam past reefs of coral, with colours flower bright.

He swam past flickering fishes, then disappeared from sight.

I asked the octopuses where he might have gone.

They just shrugged and shook their legs. I steadily swam on.

I came across a mermaid, as she combed her hair.

I found an ancient shipwreck, but couldn't see him there.

At last I found a secret cave! It looked so dark and dim,
I stayed outside and shivered. I did not dare go in.

Then in the cave I saw a glint, and guess who greeted me?

Not just one secret seahorse — a whole seahorse family!

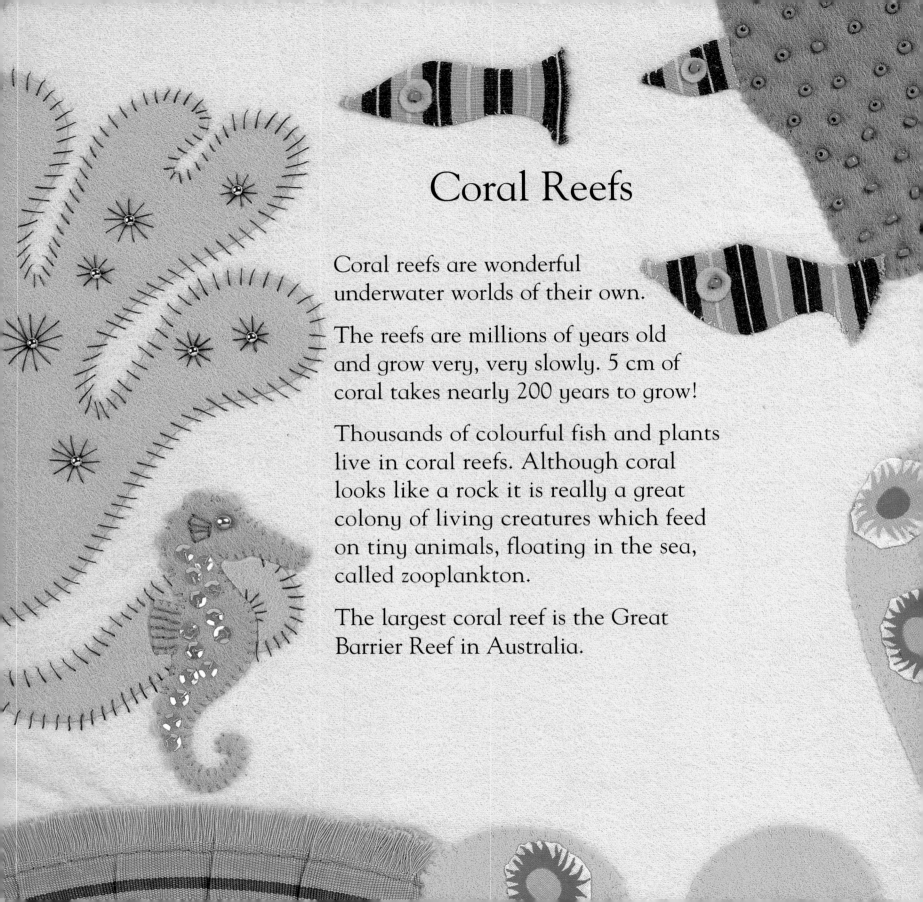

Coral Reefs

Coral reefs are wonderful underwater worlds of their own.

The reefs are millions of years old and grow very, very slowly. 5 cm of coral takes nearly 200 years to grow!

Thousands of colourful fish and plants live in coral reefs. Although coral looks like a rock it is really a great colony of living creatures which feed on tiny animals, floating in the sea, called zooplankton.

The largest coral reef is the Great Barrier Reef in Australia.

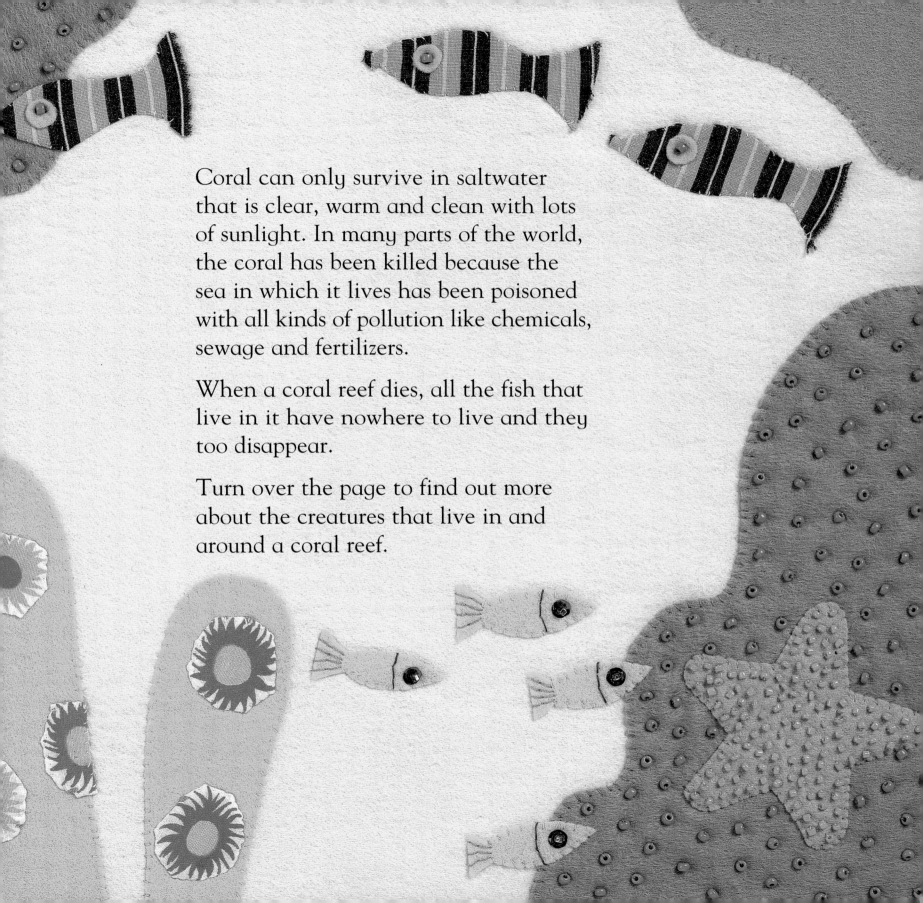

Coral can only survive in saltwater that is clear, warm and clean with lots of sunlight. In many parts of the world, the coral has been killed because the sea in which it lives has been poisoned with all kinds of pollution like chemicals, sewage and fertilizers.

When a coral reef dies, all the fish that live in it have nowhere to live and they too disappear.

Turn over the page to find out more about the creatures that live in and around a coral reef.

Creatures of the Coral Reef

Anemone
Anemones look like pretty flowers. They catch their food using the poisonous stingers on their tentacles.

Angelfish
Angelfish have flat bodies which help them squeeze through tight places to escape from fish that want to eat them.

Barracuda
Barracuda are called 'tigers of the sea' because they are fierce hunters with razor-sharp teeth.

Clown fish
Clown fish always live near anemones and help the anemones to keep their tentacles clean.

Crab
Crabs have five pairs of legs, with a big claw on the front ones. They can move in any direction, but they usually move sideways.

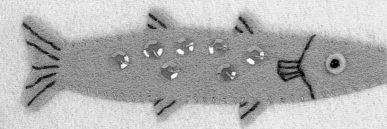

Giant clam
Giant clams live in the South Pacific and Indian oceans. The largest are bigger than 1 metre long and weigh more than 200 kilograms.

Hermit crab
Hermit crabs live in shells to protect themselves or their soft bodies. When they grow too big for one shell, they find a bigger one to move into.

Jellyfish
Most jellyfish catch their food with their stinging tentacles. Many jellyfish can give humans painful stings.

Lion fish
Lion fish are quite lazy and often just float about, waiting for their dinner to swim up to them. They use their long, sharp spines to kill.

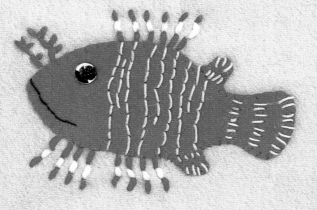

Lobster
As well as scuttling, lobsters can swim backwards by making big scooping motions with their body and tail. Most lobsters are a dark greenish colour, but some are blue.

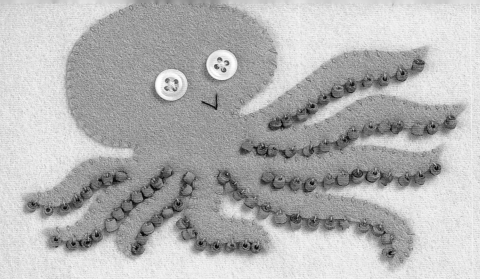

Octopus
When they sense danger, octopuses hide in rocky crevices or shoot out dark ink that clouds the water and gives them time to escape. Octopuses are very clever.

Oyster
Oysters live in shallow beds in warm ocean waters. The great pearl oyster, which makes the best pearls, lives in warm tropical seas.

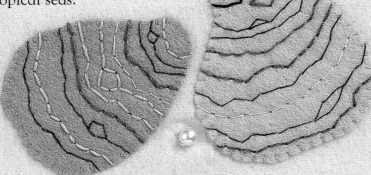

Parrotfish
Parrotfish have powerful cutting-edge beaks. They are very popular in Hawaii, and at one time, only the royal family were allowed to touch them.

Sea slug
Many people think sea slugs are the most beautiful of sea creatures, as they come in all colours and patterns.

Sea turtle
Sea turtles live a long time. They swim enormous distances to lay hundreds of eggs on special beaches.

Sea urchin
Sea urchins are covered in tough spines. The spines protect them and are also used to dig burrows.

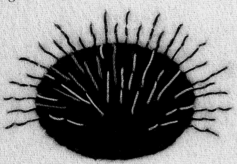

Shark
Sharks are even older than dinosaurs. They are found in seas all over the world, and can be very dangerous to humans.

Starfish (or Sea star)
Starfish have an eyespot at the very end of each arm. They use these to see light and movement.

Stingray
Stingrays whip their long tails to hurt their enemies. Their tails are covered in poisonous spines, which can kill humans.

Swordfish
The swordfish's 'sword' is actually just an extension of its upper jaw. It uses it to skewer fish to eat.

Secrets of Seahorses

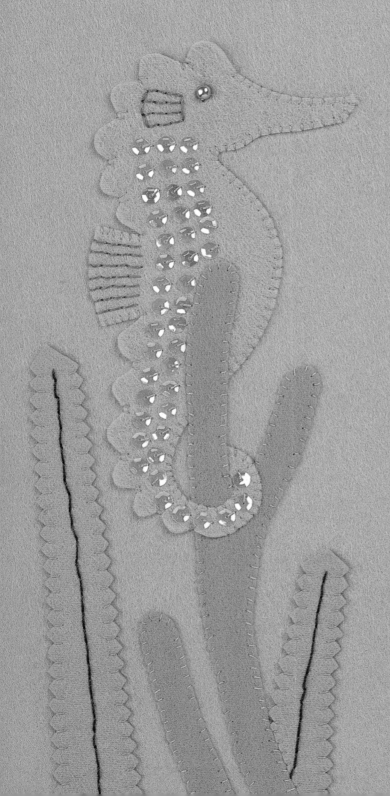

Seahorses are small fish with armoured plates all over their bodies. They move slowly by fanning their delicate fins.

They live in seaweed beds in warm water, hiding from larger fish.

Some are very small and are only an inch high, while others are one foot high.

Seahorses can move each of their eyes in different directions, making it easy for them to spot food.

They suck up food through their snouts, like sucking through a straw.

Seahorses are the only fish with tails that can hold onto things. They use their tails to cling on to sea-grass, coral or each other.

Female seahorses produce eggs, but it is the male who keeps them in a pouch in his body until they hatch after 40 to 50 days. They can have up to 400 babies at a time!

Male seahorses are the only males in the world who become pregnant like this.

Barefoot Books
Celebrating Art and Story

At Barefoot Books, we celebrate art and story with books that open the hearts and minds of children from all walks of life, inspiring them to read deeper, search further, and explore their own creative gifts. Taking our inspiration from many different cultures, we focus on themes that encourage independence of spirit, enthusiasm for learning, and acceptance of other traditions. Thoughtfully prepared by writers, artists and storytellers from all over the world, our products combine the best of the present with the best of the past to educate our children as the caretakers of tomorrow.

www.barefootbooks.com

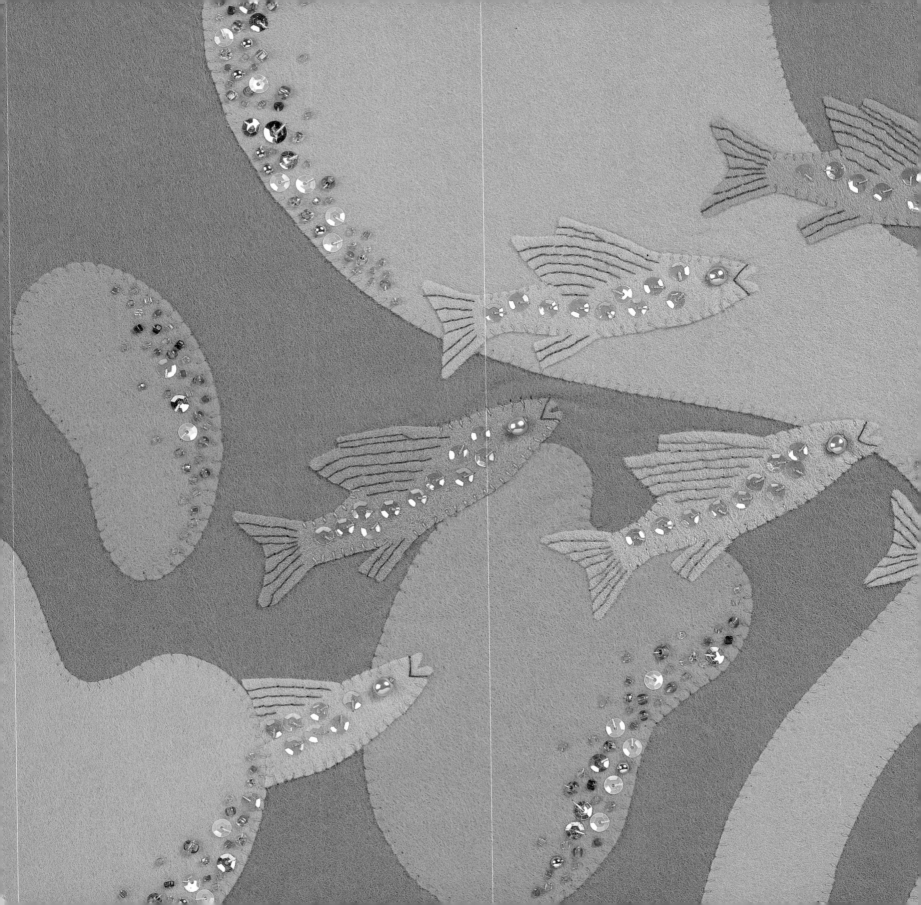